MAGIC TREE HOUSE®

#37 RHINOS AT RECESS

BY MARY POPE OSBORNE

ILLUSTRATED BY AG FORD

D0009529

A STEPPING STONE BOOK™

Random House 🏠 New York

To all those who devote their lives
to saving animals around the world

Text copyright © 2023 by Mary Pope Osborne
Cover art and interior illustrations copyright © 2023 by AG Ford

All rights reserved. Published in the United States by Random House Children's Books, a division of Penguin Random House LLC, New York. Originally published in hardcover in the United States by Random House Children's Books, a division of Penguin Random House LLC, New York, in 2023.

Random House and the colophon are registered trademarks and A Stepping Stone Book and the colophon are trademarks of Penguin Random House LLC. Magic Tree House is a registered trademark of Mary Pope Osborne; used under license.

Visit us on the Web!
rhcbooks.com
MagicTreeHouse.com

Educators and librarians, for a variety of teaching tools, visit us at
RHTeachersLibrarians.com

Library of Congress Cataloging-in-Publication Data is avilable upon request.
ISBN 978-0-593-48850-8 (trade) — ISBN 978-0-593-48851-5 (lib. bdg.) —
ISBN 978-0-593-48852-2 (ebook) — ISBN 978-0-593-48853-9 (paperback)

Printed in the United States of America
10 9 8 7 6 5 4 3 2 1

This book has been officially leveled by using the F&P Text Level Gradient™ Leveling System.

Here's what kids and grown-ups have to say about the Magic Tree House® books:

"Oh, man . . . the Magic Tree House series
is really exciting!"
—Christina

"I like the Magic Tree House series. I stay up
all night reading them. Even on school nights!"
—Peter

"Jack and Annie have opened a door to a world
of literacy that I know will continue throughout
the lives of my students."
—Deborah H.

"As a librarian, I have seen many happy young
readers coming into the library to check out
the next Magic Tree House book in the series."
—Lynne H.

Magic Tree House®

For a list of Magic Tree House® Merlin Missions and other Magic Tree House® titles, look in the back of this book.

CONTENTS

PROLOGUE

One summer day in Frog Creek, Pennsylvania, a mysterious tree house appeared in the woods. It was filled with books. A boy named Jack and his sister, Annie, found the tree house and soon discovered that it was magic. They could go to any time and place in history just by pointing to a picture in one of the books. While they were gone, no time at all passed back in Frog Creek.

Jack and Annie eventually found out that the tree house belonged to Morgan le Fay, a magical librarian from the legendary realm of Camelot.

Since then, they have traveled on many adventures in the magic tree house and completed many missions for Morgan.

On their most recent adventures, Jack and Annie have spent time with some extraordinary creatures around the world: a narwhal, a llama, a grizzly bear, and a snow leopard. Now Jack and Annie are about to set out once more to explore the wondrous world of nature.

1

RECESS IN AFRICA?

A spring wind blew across the schoolyard. The playground was bathed in morning light. Kids were shouting, tossing balls and running races.

"Jack!"

Jack was playing volleyball. He saw Annie calling to him from the edge of the court.

"I need your help, please!" she shouted.

"I'll be right back," Jack said to his teammates. He ran over to Annie.

"What's up?" he said.

"I left the folder for my science project at home,"

Annie said. "I have to give my report after recess. My teacher called Mom at work. Mom said I can go home and get it if you come with me. We have to be back in fifteen minutes, before recess ends!"

"Okay, no problem," said Jack. Their house was only a couple of blocks away. He turned to his friends. "We have to get something at home! Be back soon!"

Jack and Annie ran from the playground and started up the sidewalk toward their house.

"What's your report about?" asked Jack.

"What do you think?" said Annie.

Jack smiled. "Some kind of animal," he said. "But what is it?" Annie was an expert on animals.

"*All* kinds," said Annie. "I have to get my big folder of pictures."

Heading up their street, Jack and Annie walked by a church and the library. As they passed the Frog Creek woods, Annie grabbed Jack's arm.

"Stop! Look!" she said.

She pointed to a small gray bird sitting on a branch. The bird had a bright-red beak. Its yellow eyes were staring straight at them.

"What's that?" said Jack.

"A red-billed oxpecker," Annie said in a hushed voice. "I thought they only lived in Africa."

The bird let out a raspy cry.

"He wants us to follow him," said Annie.

"We can't. Not if you want to get your folder," said Jack. "We have just enough time to go to our house and get back to school before the end of recess."

The oxpecker cried out again. Then it spread its wings, lifted off the branch, and flew into the woods.

"We have to follow him!" said Annie.

"We can't do *both*. I told you," said Jack. "Make a choice. Your science report? Or the bird?"

The oxpecker called from the trees.

"The bird!" said Annie. She started running.

"Oh, man," said Jack. But he hurried after Annie.

The little bird kept calling, leading them on through the Frog Creek woods.

"This has to mean the tree house is there!" called Annie. "Maybe we're going all the way to Africa!"

"I guess we'll find out!" said Jack.

"Remember our other two trips to Africa?" said Annie. "The gorillas in the mountain forest? The lions in Tanzania?"

"Oh, yeah, the lions," Jack said with a shiver. They had barely escaped the lions.

Annie and Jack hurried through the woods until the oxpecker called to them from the tallest oak.

They stopped and looked up at the top of the tree.

Sunlight shone on the magic tree house.

"I guess you made the right choice!" said Jack.

"Yes, I did!" said Annie.

The oxpecker took off into the bright spring sky.

"Thank you!" Annie called after it.

Then she grabbed the rope ladder and started up. Jack followed.

When they climbed inside, Jack looked around and frowned.

"Morgan didn't send a research book," he said. "She just left the Pennsylvania book to take us back home."

"Yeah, but here's a note!" said Annie. She picked up a piece of paper from a dark corner of the tree house. She unfolded the paper and read aloud:

Journey to a grassland
With flowers and thorns,
Wildebeests, zebras,
And creatures with horns.

8

Use magic just once.
Save life, old and new.
To chase away danger,
Here's what to do:

Find a paper tree
With roots at the top.
Point to the giant. Say:
"PLEASE MAKE THEM STOP!"

"Wow. I guess we're having recess in Africa today," Annie said. "That's the only place where wildebeests and zebras live naturally—just like oxpeckers."

"And lions?" asked Jack.

Annie nodded. "Nearly all wild lions live in Africa."

"O-kay," Jack said with a sigh. He took a deep breath and looked at the rhyme.

"What's a *paper tree*?" he said.

"Hmm . . . ," said Annie. "Paper can be made from trees. So maybe it has something to do with that."

"No. It says *with roots at the top*," said Jack. "Trees only have roots at the bottom. And what does this mean: *Point to the giant*? What giant?"

"A big animal, like a gorilla or an elephant?" said Annie.

"They're big, but I wouldn't call them giants," said Jack. He looked around. "Too bad we don't have a research book."

"We'll just have to figure it out," said Annie. "Should we point to the word *grassland* and make a wish?"

"Go for it," said Jack. He handed Annie the rhyme. "But listen, when we land, don't run off like you usually do. Wait until we decide on a plan. Something we *both* agree on. Promise?"

"Sure," Annie said. "Let's go." She pointed at the word *grassland*.

"I wish we could go *there*!" she said.

The wind started to blow.

The tree house started to spin.

It spun faster and faster.

Then everything was still.

Absolutely still.

2

HEY, KIDS!

Bright sunlight poured into the tree house.

Jack heard swishing sounds and birdsong.

"We're wearing our same clothes," said Annie. They were both still dressed in T-shirts and jeans.

"Maybe we're still in the present time," said Jack.

They looked out the window together.

"It's Africa!" said Annie.

The tree house was tucked into an umbrella-like tree. Other trees and spiky-looking bushes were scattered across a grassy plain.

A warm wind rustled the high grass with a swishing sound.

"Zebras!" said Annie.

In the distance, two zebras were grazing. "And wildebeests!"

"Yep. We're definitely in Africa," said Jack. The sight of the horned wildebeests and black-and-white-striped zebras took his breath away. Then he glanced around for lions.

"Look!" said Annie.

Jack jumped. "Lions?" he said.

"No," said Annie. "Tourists!"

She pointed to a bus bumping along a dirt road that wound through the grassland.

Painted letters on the side of the bus said:

SAFARI RIDE

Passengers sat in several rows of seats in the open-air bus.

"Cool!" said Jack. He was relieved. If tourists were safe here, he and Annie must be safe, too.

The bus came to a halt. "Stopping for photos!" the driver called.

Some of the tourists jumped out to photograph the zebras and wildebeests.

"We're definitely still in our time," said Annie. "They're all using cell phones to take pictures."

"Right," said Jack.

"Come on! Let's join them!" said Annie.

"The Safari Ride?" said Jack.

"Yes!" said Annie. "I've always wanted to go on a safari and see the animals."

"Don't be silly," said Jack. "We can't just appear out of nowhere and hop on the bus. They'll wonder where we came from. Let's stick to our mission."

He looked at their rhyme again. He repeated the second and third verses:

Use magic just once.
Save life, old and new.
To chase away danger,
Here's what to do:

Find a paper tree
With roots at the top.
Point to the giant. Say:
"PLEASE MAKE THEM STOP!"

"Okay. The good news is we can use magic in case of danger," said Annie.

"But how do we use it?" said Jack.

"Well, it says we have to find a *paper tree* with roots at the top," said Annie. "Then we point to a giant and—"

"Stop. We still don't know what a *paper tree* is!" said Jack. "What does it have to do with a giant? And who are *them*? What do we want *them* to stop doing?"

"I don't know," said Annie, heaving a sigh.

"Nothing makes sense," said Jack.

"Don't worry," said Annie. "Let's just join the Safari Ride and have some fun! And we can ask the other people about *paper trees*."

"Seriously, we can't join them," said Jack. "The driver will wonder why we're here alone in the middle of nowhere. It'll turn into a big deal, and then we'll be in trouble."

"I'll think of something to say," said Annie.

"Back onboard!" the driver called to his passengers.

"Hurry! The bus is about to leave!" said Annie. She scrambled down the rope ladder.

"I just told you we can't join them!" called Jack. But Annie was already heading toward the bus.

"Oh, brother!" Jack stuffed Morgan's note into his back pocket and hurried after Annie.

As he stepped into the tall grass, the Safari Ride bus started moving.

"Wait! Hey, wait!" Annie shouted. She started running after the bus.

"Annie, hold on!" Jack called after her. "Forget it! It's too far away!"

Annie stopped, gasping for breath. She and Jack watched the safari bus bump down the dirt road. Soon it disappeared behind a thicket of trees and bushes.

"Annie, I told you, we have to stick to our mission!" said Jack.

Annie looked down. "I'm sorry. I got carried away," she said.

"We have to make a plan," said Jack. "Something we *both* agree on."

"Okay. Okay," said Annie.

Jack sighed and pushed his glasses into place. He looked around. "So what now?" he said.

The zebras and wildebeests still grazed in the distance.

Loud chirping and clicking sounds came from the grass. Dragonflies darted among purple wildflowers.

Croaking sounds came from a muddy creek. A swarm of mosquitoes danced in the air.

"Hey, what's that?" said Annie.

"What's what?" said Jack.

"*That.*" Annie walked over to some weeds. She bent down and picked up a booklet.

"*South African Game Reserve,*" she read aloud

from the cover. "Someone on the Safari Ride must have dropped this."

"Let me see," said Jack.

Annie handed him the booklet. Jack read the front page:

A number of African game reserves, like this one, protect some of the largest animals on earth, such as elephants, giraffes, and black rhinos.

"Oh, wow! We landed in a game reserve!" said Annie. "They protect animals here! That's *so* great!"

"Yeah, it is," said Jack. He kept reading:

Reserve rangers guard the grasslands and take visitors on safari rides. Sometimes the rangers risk their lives to protect animals from deadly danger.

"Deadly danger," repeated Jack. "Like what? Lions?"

"Maybe," said Annie. "Keep going."

Before Jack could read more, the rumble of an engine came from behind them. He and Annie quickly turned around.

An old jeep was bouncing up the dirt road.

The vehicle stopped near Jack and Annie. A young man and woman jumped out. They wore tan uniforms with name badges.

"Hey, kids!" the man shouted. "What are you doing out here all by yourselves?"

3

JOMO AND SHANI

Jack froze. He didn't know what to say.

Annie walked over to the two people. "Hi! We're Jack and Annie. We're visiting the game reserve. Do you work here?"

"Yes," said the woman. She pointed to her name badge. It said RANGER SHANI. "I'm Shani. And this is Jomo. We're both reserve rangers."

"Wow," said Annie. "I'd love to be a reserve ranger!"

"Maybe someday you will be," said Shani.

"Back to my question: What are you two doing out here by yourselves?" Jomo asked sternly.

"We—uh—" Jack stammered.

"*That*," said Annie, pointing to the Safari Ride booklet in Jack's hand. "We were doing that. But they drove off without us."

"It wasn't the driver's fault," Jack said quickly. "We—we were just too far away when the bus took off. We didn't make it back in time."

"They didn't miss you?" said Shani.

Annie shook her head.

"Not even your parents?"

"Well, to be honest, they weren't with us," said Annie. "They . . . they're off doing some research. So we—at least I—wanted to go on a Safari Ride."

"You know, your story really doesn't make much sense," said Jomo, squinting at them.

"I know," agreed Annie, "but . . ." She shrugged.

"Whatever happened, this is not a safe place to be wandering around alone," said Shani. "The bus will come back this way soon. We'll wait here with you until you get back on."

Uh-oh, thought Jack. The rangers would soon find out they had never been on the Safari Ride.

"Good. So what are *you* guys up to?" said Annie, changing the subject.

"We're searching for Rosie," said Shani.

"Oh," said Annie. "Is Rosie a kid or a grown-up?"

"She's a black rhino," said Shani.

Jack and Annie laughed. "A rhino named Rosie?" said Annie, grinning. "That's funny."

"Yes. But it's *not* funny that no one's seen her for a week," said Shani. "She was about to give birth."

"A *baby* rhino!" said Annie. "Aww. I'd love to meet one."

"I'm afraid you can't," said Jomo. "A mother rhino can be dangerous."

"Why? Are they meat-eaters?" asked Jack.

"No, rhinos are plant-eaters," Annie said.

"They are," said Shani. "But they can be very protective. If a rhino thinks you might harm her baby, she'll probably charge at you."

"She could ram you with her head and crush you," said Jomo. "*Or* stab you with her horn."

"And rhinos can run faster than we do," Annie said matter-of-factly. "Up to thirty miles an hour."

Jomo smiled. "You know a lot about rhinos, Annie," he said.

"Annie knows a lot about *lots* of animals," Jack said.

"I do," said Annie. "But now I'm worried about Rosie and her baby."

"We are, too," said Shani. "Rosie's one of our favorites. She was brought to the reserve as an orphan years ago. We've watched her grow up. We're eager to welcome her calf into our lives."

"Are you afraid another animal might hurt them?" asked Jack. "Like a lion?"

"No. We're more concerned about poachers," said Shani.

"What kind of animal is a *poacher*?" asked Annie.

"A *human* animal," Jomo said. "Poachers kill rhinos for money. They sell their horns for large amounts."

"Oh, that's terrible!" Annie said.

"It is," said Shani. "But our job is to *save* the rhinos. We just wish the rest of the world felt the same way."

Suddenly a tiny creature with a long tail sprang from the back of the jeep. It bounced off the ground and landed in Jomo's arms.

"Ahh! Speedy! You hitched a ride with us!" said Jomo.

Speedy had a tiny head with bat-like ears and huge, round eyes.

"A bush baby!" cried Annie.

"Speedy's the mascot at our camp dining hall," said Shani. "During the day, he likes to hide in the back of our vehicles and nap."

The bush baby made funny squeaky sounds.

"Ohhh. He's so cute," cooed Annie. "Can I hold him?"

"Better not. He might nip you," said Jomo.

"I'm not afraid. Please," said Annie. She held out her arms.

"Okay. Speedy, be good," said Jomo. He gently placed Speedy in Annie's hands.

Annie cradled the tiny bush baby. He was no bigger than a kitten.

"Hey, little guy," Annie said. "Your fur's so soft and nice."

Speedy swiveled his head around to look at her. He made a croaking sound.

Annie laughed. "He says he agrees," she said to Jack. "Bush babies are tiny primates who live only in Africa. Did you know that?"

Before Jack could say no, a crackling radio noise came from inside the jeep.

"Code red! Code red!" a man's voice shouted.

"Oh, no! Grab it," said Shani.

Jomo reached into the jeep and grabbed the radio receiver. "We're here! Go ahead!" he shouted.

Through the radio static, the man shouted back, "Chopper sighting! West Gate! Code red!"

"On our way!" Jomo yelled into the radio receiver. He looked at Shani. "We have to go. *Now!*"

4

SPEEDY, SLOW DOWN!

"Got it," said Shani. The two rangers jumped back into their jeep.

"Come on, Jack!" said Annie. Holding Speedy, she started to climb into the jeep, too.

"Oh, no, no, no, kids. You can't go with us," said Shani.

"Why not?" asked Annie.

"Too dangerous!" said Jomo.

"We don't mind danger!" said Annie.

Jack hung back. "Wait, what kind of danger?" he asked.

"Poachers," said Shani. "They might spot Rosie. We have to race to the west side of the reserve before their chopper lands."

"What's a chopper?" asked Annie.

"A helicopter," Jack said.

"Yes, sometimes poachers use helicopters and carry heavy weapons," said Shani.

Jomo started the jeep engine. "The Safari Ride will be back soon," he said. "Please wait here for the bus. Don't wander the bush."

"We'll see you back at the camp!" said Shani.

The jeep lurched forward.

"Wait! You forgot Speedy!" Annie shouted.

The rangers didn't hear her as their jeep roared away.

Speedy made sad, chirpy sounds.

"I'm sorry, Speedy. They had to go save Rosie," Annie said to the tiny primate. She looked at Jack. "I really wanted to go with them. Didn't you?"

"Uh, no. It sounded super-dangerous," said

Jack. "Shani and Jomo are trained to handle these situations."

"But I wanted to save Rosie, too," said Annie.

"I know you did," said Jack. "But let's just do what they told us and wait here for the Safari Ride to come back."

"You didn't want to join the ride before," said Annie.

"I know, but it's different now," Jack said. "We can tell the driver that Jomo and Shani told us to get onboard and meet them back at their camp."

Annie sighed. "So we just stand here and wait?"

"Yes. And we take care of Speedy," said Jack.

"Okay. That's important, too," said Annie. She hugged the tiny bush baby.

Jack looked at their booklet again. He read aloud:

Never before has it been so important to keep large rare animals alive on

33

earth. In a number of African nature reserves, rangers risk their lives to save endangered elephants and rhinos.

"I'd love to train to be a reserve ranger someday," said Annie. "Wouldn't you?"

"Um . . . maybe," said Jack. He looked around. He felt hot, sweaty, and itchy. He waved the booklet to shoo away mosquitoes whining around his head.

"You okay?" said Annie.

"It's too buggy here near the creek," said Jack. "Let's walk up the road toward those trees. The bus will come back that way."

"Sure," said Annie. "And maybe we'll find out what Morgan means by a *paper tree*."

"Maybe," said Jack.

He and Annie started up the dusty dirt road. As they walked, Speedy perched on Annie's shoulder.

Jack turned the pages of the booklet. He read aloud:

For more than thirty million years, rhinos and their ancestors have survived ice ages, earthquakes, floods, and volcanoes.

"Rhinos and their *ancestors*?" said Annie. "What does that mean?"

"All creatures have ancestors that go back through time," said Jack. "Like our great-great-great-grandmothers, grandfathers, and parents. You know."

"Oh, yeah, our family history," said Annie. "Uncle Josh is making a chart of that."

"Look. Here's a great-great-ancestor chart for rhinos," said Jack. He showed Annie the chart in the booklet. At the top was an illustration of a prehistoric rhino. At the bottom of the chart was a present-day rhino.

Jack read:

Modern-day rhinoceroses are descended from the family of prehistoric rhinos, which includes the Paraceratherium (say pa-ruh-seh-ruh-THEE-ree-um).

"Whew. Hard word," said Annie.

"Just look at this monster," said Jack. He pointed to the drawing at the top of the chart. It showed a huge, long-necked creature. To illustrate the creature's size, there was a tiny person drawn next to it. Jack read more:

This ancient rhinoceros was the largest land mammal that ever lived. The creature weighed at least five times as much as a rhino of today. It was a plant-eater that mainly ate leaves and grass.

"Cool, a plant-eater," said Annie.

"Yep. But I wouldn't want it to step on me," said Jack. He kept reading:

The armor of the rhino family has protected the animals for millions of years. But humans have found ways to kill rhinos, and they are critically endangered. Some experts worry that black rhinos could disappear from Africa within ten years.

"What? Only ten years?" cried Annie. "That's horrible! Rhinos have been around for over thirty million years! And now they might disappear from Africa in just *ten years*? I hate that!"

"Me too," said Jack.

Suddenly Speedy let out a shrill whistle. He leapt out of Annie's arms onto the ground. He frantically hopped around, jabbering.

"Speedy, what's wrong?" said Annie.

The tiny bush baby took flying leaps up the road. He headed toward the bushes and umbrella-like trees.

"Wait! Wait! Speedy!" Annie called. "Speedy, slow down! We have to keep you safe!" She started running after the bush baby.

"Come on, Jack!" Annie shouted.

Jack stuck the booklet into his pocket. Then he raced after Annie and Speedy up the dirt road.

5

DON'T MOVE!

Speedy stayed far ahead of Jack and Annie. He dashed into the thicket.

"Speedy! Where are you?" Annie called.

The bush baby croaked from inside the bushes.

"Come out from there!" said Annie. She tried pushing through the closely packed shrubs.

"Oww! Oww!" Annie cried, jumping back. She rubbed her arms. "That really hurt!"

"No wonder!" said Jack. "Look!"

Jutting out between the feathery leaves of the

bushes were dagger-like thorns. Each spike was three or four inches long.

"Yikes," said Annie.

"We can't go in there," said Jack. "We'll get stabbed to death."

"But what about Speedy?" said Annie.

"I don't know," said Jack. "Maybe he'll—"

"Shh! Listen," said Annie.

Jack held his breath.

Loud snuffling and snorting noises came from the thornbushes.

"That doesn't sound like Speedy," Annie said.

Jack shook his head. "It's not Speedy," he said.

"So what is it?" whispered Annie.

The snuffling and snorting grew louder.

Annie carefully tried to pull back a thorny branch. Jack grabbed her arm.

"Don't," he whispered. "Something's hiding in there. Something way bigger than a bush baby."

"Like what?" whispered Annie.

"I don't know," whispered Jack. "Just back up. Slowly. One step at a time."

"But Speedy—" started Annie.

"Now!" Jack whispered.

The two of them carefully stepped back.

A growling sound came from the bushes.

Jack's heart pounded as he looked around. They could run down the dirt road—or across the grassy plain. But a hungry animal could chase them and catch them.

His eyes rested on a tree near the bushes. Beneath the leafy top were bare branches.

"Let's climb that tree," he said. "We can wait there till the Safari Ride comes back."

"What about Speedy?" said Annie.

"We'll figure that out once we're safe," said Jack.

The bushes started to shake. Jack heard twigs and branches snap.

"Go! Now!" said Jack.

Jack and Annie dashed to the tree.

"Hurry!" Jack said.

Annie grabbed a limb and pulled herself up.

Jack followed, lifting himself onto a branch near her. As he tried to climb higher, his hand was stuck by thorns.

"Ouch!" he cried.

"Are you okay?" Annie said.

"Watch out! There are thorns here, too! They're near the top," Jack said.

Jack and Annie settled on bare branches just below the crown of the tree.

"Look!" said Annie.

A huge head emerged from the thicket.

The head had upright ears and a long horn growing from its snout.

"Oh, man," Jack whispered.

"A rhino!" said Annie.

The rhino grunted and lumbered out from the bushes. Its wide, bulky body was covered with wrinkled dark-gray skin.

"A *real* rhino," Annie said.

"Rhinos are dangerous, don't forget," said Jack.

"Where's Speedy?" said Annie.

"Shh! Don't call out to him," Jack whispered. "Remember Jomo said a rhino can crush you or stab you."

The rhino moved forward on thick, heavy legs. It swung its head from side to side.

Jack held his breath, afraid the animal might see them. "Don't move," he whispered.

"Rhinos can't see well," Annie said softly. "They rely on hearing and smell."

"Then don't talk," whispered Jack.

"But do you think Speedy's safe?" Annie whispered.

"Shh! Quiet!"

The rhino turned its gaze in their direction. It twitched its ears, as if trying to hear them. It snorted, as if trying to smell them.

Can a rhino knock down a tree? Jack wondered. *Is a rhino the "danger" in Morgan's rhyme?*

Jack quietly pulled Morgan's note from his back pocket. He read to himself:

Use magic just once.
Save life, old and new.
To chase away danger,
Here's what to do:

Find a paper tree
With roots at the top.
Point to the giant. Say:
"PLEASE MAKE THEM STOP!"

The words still made no sense! The tree they had climbed was definitely not a *paper tree*. And who were *the giant* and *them*?

He put the rhyme back into his pocket.

The rhino turned its head. It sniffed the air.

"Listen! I hear Speedy!" Annie whispered.

Jack heard jabbering coming from the brush.

Suddenly the thornbushes parted—and out came Speedy!

He was riding on the back of a baby rhino!

6

CODE RED!

"Speedy!" Annie whispered loudly.

Speedy looked up at the tree where Jack and Annie were hiding. He jumped off the rhino calf and leapt to the tree. He scuttled up to them.

"You're safe!" Annie whispered, hugging the bush baby.

Speedy jabbered excitedly.

"I know, a baby rhino! It's so sweet!" Annie said to him.

"Not so loud," whispered Jack. "That big rhino must be Rosie. The little one is her calf."

"I know!" said Annie.

The baby rhino was only about two feet tall. She hadn't grown a horn yet. But she looked just like her mother. She had wrinkled dark-gray skin, a large head, and upright ears.

"She's a miniature Rosie. A Rosita!" said Annie.

"A what?" whispered Jack.

"Rosita—it means *little Rose* in Spanish," said Annie.

"Shh! Rosie's coming back," whispered Jack. "Remember a mother rhino can be dangerous!"

The mother rhino walked over to her calf and nuzzled her. Then she lay down in the grass on her side.

"Oh, yeah . . . she's sooo dangerous," Annie said, grinning.

"Seriously," Jack said. "We have to stay in the tree."

While Rosie rested, her calf climbed halfway onto her back. The baby pawed her mother, as if trying to get her to play.

Annie giggled softly, and Jack couldn't help

grinning. A baby rhino might be the cutest animal in the world, he thought.

Rosie finally grunted and heaved herself up. She ate some grass. Then she began moving away from the trees.

The calf followed on her stumpy little legs. The two rhinos rounded the cluster of bushes.

Jack and Annie couldn't see them anymore.

"Now we have to climb down," said Annie. "So we can track them and tell the rangers where they are."

"Okay," said Jack. "But we have to stay far away from them. Remember rhinos can move fast. Don't let her see you. And, Speedy"—he spoke sternly to the bush baby—"don't talk!"

Speedy swiveled his head and looked at Annie.

"Just whisper," she said. "Come on!"

Speedy hopped onto Annie's back. He put his little arms around her neck. Annie carefully climbed down from the tree. Jack followed.

They crept over the grass and rounded the thorny thicket. They stood at a safe distance and watched the two rhinos.

Rosie and her calf had ambled down to the creek. They both sank into the muddy water.

Jack and Annie watched the rhinos wallow in the mud. Wildebeests grazed in the distance. Zebras roamed the tall grass.

Overhead, birds with long, slender wings swooped through the blue sky.

It was a perfect scene, Jack thought. Beautiful and peaceful. All the creatures were doing what they were born to do.

"Look at that," said Annie, pointing at the sky. "Is that a bird?"

Jack squinted in the sunlight. He saw something in the distance flying toward them.

Speedy started jabbering wildly.

"That's not a bird," said Jack.

"A small plane?" said Annie.

As the thing in the sky drew closer, they could hear whapping and chopping sounds.

Jack felt sick. "It's not a plane," he said.

"What, then?" said Annie.

"A helicopter," said Jack. "A chopper."

"Oh, no! Poachers!" cried Annie. "Code red!!"

"Yes!" said Jack. "This must be the chopper that Jomo and Shani were after."

Speedy whistled and shrieked.

"Rosie! We have to save her!" said Annie.

"I know!" said Jack.

"How? How?" Annie said.

"Get her to a hiding place!" said Jack.

"In the thornbushes?" said Annie.

"Better if we get them under that tree we were in!" said Jack. "The leaves might keep them from being seen from the sky!"

"How do we do that?" cried Annie.

"I don't know!" said Jack.

"Wait," said Annie. "What if we yell at Rosie's

baby? We make Rosie mad at us. She chases us. We run. Her baby follows."

"We can't outrun a rhino," said Jack. "You said they can run thirty miles an hour!"

"We'll get a head start!" said Annie. "And we'll lead Rosie and her baby back to our tree! Let's do it!"

The terrible chopper noise was growing louder.

"Jack, it's the only plan we've got," said Annie.

Jack looked from the tree to the helicopter to the rhino.

"Right. Okay," he said. "Let's go!"

7

MOVE, BABY! MOVE!

Clutching Speedy, Annie ran down toward the muddy creek.

Jack ran with her.

"Rosie! Rosita!" Annie yelled. "Get out of the water!"

"Come on, you two!" Jack shouted.

Speedy shrieked and whistled.

The baby rhino seemed to smile at them.

The mother lifted her huge head out of the water. She stared darkly at Jack and Annie.

The helicopter was getting closer.

"Hurry, Rosie! Come out!" yelled Annie. "Try to catch us!"

Rosie heaved herself up to a standing position in the creek. Muddy water poured off her thick body.

"Get ready to run!" Jack said to Annie.

"Wait! What about the baby?" said Annie.

The calf was still wallowing in the mud.

"Rosita, get out! Run after us!" called Annie.

"Move, baby! Move!" shouted Jack. He clapped his hands at the calf.

Suddenly the baby bounced out of the creek.

Annie rushed to the small, muddy rhino. "Good for you!" she said.

"Annie, watch out for Rosie!" shouted Jack.

Quicker than he'd expected, Rosie had moved out of the water onto the grass.

She started slowly toward Annie. She pawed the ground and made a growling sound.

"Whoa! Go! Go!" Jack called to Annie.

Jack and Annie took off running as fast as they could.

They raced back toward the trees and thorny bushes. When Jack looked over his shoulder, he saw Rosie galloping after them. Her legs bounded across the grass.

The calf's stumpy little legs moved fast, too.

The chopping sounds of the helicopter grew louder.

"Climb back up the tree!" Jack shouted at Annie.

They ran to the umbrella-like tree. Annie let go of Speedy, and the bush baby leapt into the branches.

Jack and Annie climbed after him. The three of them sat on bare branches. They were hidden by the thick cover of overhead leaves.

The mother rhino followed them to the tree. She stood below them and huffed and snorted.

She's really mad, thought Jack. But at least she was hidden under the leafy canopy.

"Stay there, Rosie!" Annie cried. She turned to Jack. "Where's her baby?"

"Over there," said Jack.

The calf hadn't followed Rosie all the way to the tree. She was romping in the grass.

"Oh, no! Rosita!" Annie shouted. "Come over here!"

Annie's voice could hardly be heard above the roar of the chopper.

"What should we do?" Annie cried.

"I don't know!" said Jack.

"Maybe the safari bus will come back soon! Or Jomo and Shani!" said Annie. She sounded like she might cry.

The helicopter could be seen clearly now. Its spinning blades made whirring, chopping sounds.

"The poachers will see the baby!" Annie said.

As the helicopter circled the area, the rhino calf kept playing. She could easily be spotted in the open.

"I have to get her," said Annie.

"No, you can't!" said Jack.

"The poachers will see her! I have to help!" said Annie. She was in tears.

"Don't climb down, Annie! Please!" said Jack. "Rosie won't understand. She'll attack you!"

The helicopter hovered above the dirt road. The spinning blades made a deafening sound.

Slowly the machine started to descend.

"They're coming down!" cried Annie.

As the chopper drew close to the ground, its blades stirred up a cloud of dust.

"They're landing!" said Annie. "I have to go down and protect Rosie and her baby! They're in terrible danger!"

"Wait, Annie! That's it! Morgan's rhyme!" said Jack.

He pulled the rhyme out of his pocket. He shouted Morgan's words above the roar of the chopper:

To chase away danger,
Here's what to do:

Find a paper tree
With roots at the top.
Point to the giant. Say:
"PLEASE MAKE THEM STOP!"

"We need a paper tree!" cried Jack. "Paper tree, paper tree," he repeated, looking around in a panic.

The helicopter had landed. The blades were slowing down.

"We're out of time!" said Annie.

"Hold on!" said Jack.

He pulled the safari booklet out of his pocket. His hands shook as he turned the pages. He found the chart of rhino ancestors.

He stared at the giant creature at the top of the chart and its descendants below.

"Jack! What are you doing?" said Annie. "They're here!"

"That's it!" he said. "The rhino *family tree!*"

"What?" said Annie.

"A tree made of paper!" said Jack. "With roots at the top! It's not a real tree! It's this chart of rhino ancestors! The *rhino* family tree!"

"Oh, wow!" said Annie.

"*Roots* can mean *ancestors,*" said Jack. He pointed to the top of the rhino family tree. "And there's the giant!"

He glanced up. Two men in dark masks were climbing out of the helicopter.

Jack held up the illustration of the rhino family tree. *"Now!"* he said.

Together Jack and Annie shouted at the drawing of the giant prehistoric creature at the top of the page: "PLEASE MAKE THEM STOP!"

And then . . . something magnificent started to happen.

8

THE GIANT GREAT-ANCESTOR

A blinding light flashed over the grasslands.

The wind blew. Birds cried out.

Trees and bushes trembled.

Speedy swiveled his head to look around. He let out a shriek.

Jack and Annie turned to look behind them.

A creature was rising up from the blowing tall yellow grass. He had a massive head with upright ears. He had a thick neck, as long as a giraffe's!

Slowly the creature rose to his full height. He stood as tall as a two-story building.

The body of the ancient creature was covered with hairless gray skin that looked like armor. His four legs were as thick as huge tree trunks.

Rosie and her baby froze in place.

The masked poachers stopped, too.

Annie and Jack gasped.

"The rhino's great-ancestor," said Annie, *"from thirty million years ago!"*

"Oh, man," Jack whispered. "This isn't real."

"It's real, totally real," said Annie. "And it's magic."

The prehistoric rhino started moving toward them, his huge feet crushing the tall grass.

As the creature came closer, his head swayed from right to left. He looked at the two smaller rhinos and the helicopter parked on the ground.

Then he stopped and glared down at the two masked men. The giant let out a low, deep sound—a strange bellowing that seemed to come from a world before the time of humans.

The creature's voice grew louder and louder, until its booming roar shattered the air.

The prehistoric giant started moving toward the poachers. Faster and faster. His thundering footfalls shook the ground.

The poachers howled in terror. They dashed to the chopper. They scrambled back into the cockpit.

The rotor blades started spinning.

The helicopter lifted off the ground, rocking from side to side.

A whirlwind of dust blew up from the dirt road.

The chopper rose shakily through the dust. It almost tipped over.

The ancient rhino looked up and bellowed again.

The fleeing helicopter rose higher. It turned and sputtered away across the sky.

The chopper was gone. The grasslands seemed stunned into a watchful silence.

The birds and frogs were quiet.

67

Rosie and her calf didn't move.

Jack and Annie were speechless.

Speedy broke the stillness. He slipped out of Annie's arms.

Jabbering excitedly, he jumped down onto the baby rhino's back. From there, he leapt onto Rosie's head. From there, he scrambled onto the back of the ancient rhino.

Speedy hugged the giant's neck. He made happy noises, as if welcoming the ancient creature to this world.

The huge rhino lowered his head and looked around again. Then he started moving toward Rosie and her baby.

Jack held his breath, afraid for their safety. But as the giant stepped closer to them, Rosie and Rosita walked toward him as if to thank him.

The giant rhino leaned over. He nuzzled Rosie's head with his own. Then the three of them stood calmly together.

"Let's go down. It's safe now," Annie said.

Jack nodded. He felt the same. The peace among the rhinos seemed to extend everywhere.

Jack and Annie climbed down from the tree. They slowly approached the rhino family.

Annie stroked the baby's head. Then she rested her hand on Rosie.

"Hi there. This is your great-ancestor," she said softly. "He saved you."

Jack reached out and touched the leathery skin of the ancient ancestor.

The giant gazed at Jack and Annie with soft, dark eyes. He dipped his large, curved head down to touch their heads.

Then the creature stood up straight, looming over them all.

"Thanks for saving them," said Annie, looking up at him.

"Yes . . . thank you," Jack murmured. "Thank you for helping us."

69

The giant seemed to nod. Then he turned and began walking away.

Speedy climbed down from the creature's back and jumped into Annie's arms.

Jack, Annie, Rosie, and her calf stood together. They watched the prehistoric rhino stop for a moment. He nibbled leaves from the top of the tallest umbrella-like tree. Then he kept plodding across the yellow plain.

They watched the creature move through the tall, swaying grass until he vanished into the bright African sunshine.

"Good-bye," Annie said softly.

Jack didn't speak. He was still in shock.

Suddenly the sound of an engine came from behind them.

Jack and Annie turned and saw the rangers' jeep rumbling down the road.

"Shani and Jomo!" cried Annie. "They're back!"

The jeep came to a halt. The two rangers leapt out.

"Get away from the rhinos, kids!" Jomo shouted. "You're in great danger!"

"No. No, we're not," said Jack, finding his voice. "Actually, we're fine. We're *all* totally fine."

9

MESSAGE RECEIVED

"Look! We found Rosie and her baby!" Annie shouted. She patted Rosie's thick gray hide.

The rangers walked slowly and carefully toward Jack, Annie, and the two rhinos.

"I named her baby Rosita," said Annie.

"Ah, wonderful. She looks to be about a week old," said Shani.

"Where did you find them?" asked Jomo.

"They found us," said Jack. "They came out from the bushes." He pointed to the thicket.

"And Rosie didn't bother you?" said Jomo.

"No, not at all," said Annie. "We watched them take a mud bath. Then they followed us back here. And then . . . well, we all became good friends."

"What happened to you?" Jack asked the rangers.

"We went on a wild-goose chase," said Shani. "No sightings of a chopper near the West Gate. But we heard it was spotted over this area. Did you see it?"

"Yes," Annie said simply.

"You did?" said Shani. "What happened?"

"It landed," said Jack. "Right here."

"What? It landed *here*?" said Jomo.

"Yep," Jack said.

"Oh, my gosh! What happened?" asked Shani. "Did the poachers see Rosie?"

"Yep. But we convinced them to leave her alone, and her baby, too," said Annie.

"How—how in the world did you do that?" asked Shani.

"Uh . . . well, we just shared some information with them," Jack said. He held up the booklet.

"We taught them that the rhino family has been on earth for at least thirty million years," said Annie. "So basically rhinos have as much right to be here as we do."

Jomo and Shani looked confused. "And—the poachers listened to you?" said Jomo.

Jack shrugged. "Somehow they seemed to get the message," he said.

"Yep. Message received," said Annie. "Now we just hope they'll tell other poachers what they learned here."

"I can't believe this," Jomo said, shaking his head.

"It sounds like a miracle," said Shani.

"It was, sort of," said Jack.

"Oh, look. There's your bus," said Jomo, pointing down the road.

The Safari Ride was bumping along the road in the distance.

"Great. They've probably been very worried about you," said Shani.

"Do you mind if we leave you here?" said Jomo. "We have to get a transport crew to help haul Rosie and her calf back to our camp."

"Oh, no, we don't mind," said Jack. He was relieved. Now the rangers wouldn't find out they'd never been on the bus.

"The other rangers will be overjoyed to see her," said Shani. "And her baby!"

"Great," said Annie, "and don't forget to take Speedy with you!"

"Oh, we won't!" said Shani. "We're sorry we left him behind. Thanks for taking good care of him."

Annie gave the bush baby one last hug. She whispered in his ear.

Speedy jabbered softly to her.

Annie whispered again.

Speedy jabbered again.

"Sorry, guys. We should hurry," said Jomo.

"Oh, sure. Bye, Speedy," said Annie. She gave the bush baby to Shani.

"Thanks for . . . well, for whatever you said to the poachers," said Shani.

"I can hardly believe they just left," said Jomo.

"We hardly believe it ourselves," said Jack.

"Well, thank you," said Shani. She and Jomo walked back to their jeep and climbed inside.

The jeep started up. It wheeled around and bounced away over the dirt road.

Jack looked over his shoulder. "The bus is getting close," he said to Annie. He put the booklet into his pocket. "We have to go home."

"Bye, Rosita," said Annie. She put her arms around the baby rhino and gave her a hug. "Be a good girl."

The baby looked as if she was smiling at Annie.

"Bye, Mama," Annie said to Rosie. "Your baby is beautiful. Congratulations. Wait right here for the transport team. They'll take you to your friends at the camp."

"Bye, Rosie and Rosita," said Jack. Then he surprised himself. He leaned over and kissed Rosie on the side of her leathery gray head.

"I hope you live a long, happy life," he murmured.

The rhino grunted, but in a warm, friendly way. Jack felt tears come to his eyes.

"Okay, let's go!" Jack said, clearing his throat. "We have to hurry!"

Jack and Annie turned away from the rhinos and started running in the opposite direction from the bus. They ran down the dirt road. They dashed through the tall yellow grass.

They ran to the rope ladder. Annie climbed up first. Jack followed.

Inside the tree house, they looked out the window. The Safari Ride had stopped not far from Rosie and her baby.

From the open-air bus, tourists were taking pictures of the two rhinos. Jack heard cries of wonder, oohs and aahs.

"That's how it should be," said Annie. "All humans should love rhinos and tell their friends to love rhinos, too."

"Yep," said Jack. "I hope that keeps happening for a long time."

"Like thirty million more years," said Annie.

"At least," said Jack. "Ready?"

He picked up the Pennsylvania book. He pointed at the picture of the Frog Creek woods.

"I wish we could go there!" he said.

The wind started to blow.

The tree house started to spin.

It spun faster and faster.

Then everything was still.

Absolutely still.

10

A Better Idea

Morning sunlight warmed the woods. Birdsong filled the air.

No time at all had passed in Frog Creek.

"We have just enough time to get back to recess," said Jack.

"Good," said Annie.

They climbed down the rope ladder and started through the woods.

"That was an amazing adventure," said Annie.

"Yeah, it really was," said Jack. He stopped.

"But wait . . . did it really happen? I mean that prehistoric rhino?"

"What? You're asking that *now*?" said Annie. "After a million trips in the magic tree house?"

Jack laughed and kept walking. "Yeah, but it was so incredible."

"It was real," said Annie. "We had eyewitnesses. Rosie, Rosita, Speedy. And the poachers!"

"Oh, yeah," said Jack, "sure." He shook his head. "Great witnesses."

"Seriously," said Annie.

"Hey, I have a question," said Jack. "Before you gave Speedy to the rangers, what were you two whispering about?"

"I said, *Be good, and don't tell anyone our secret,*" said Annie.

"Oh, yeah?" said Jack, smiling. "And what did Speedy answer?"

"Well. You know Speedy," said Annie. "He

said, *Forget it. Of course I'm going to tell the other bush babies and the zebras, wildebeests, lions, elephants, frogs, mosquitoes, and—*"

"Okay, okay," said Jack. He smiled.

"*—and all things in the grasslands,*" Annie added. "And I said, *Yes, tell them all. And he said, They'll love the story. And furthermore—*"

"Okay!" said Jack, laughing. "Enough."

Jack and Annie came out of the Frog Creek woods and started down the street toward their school.

"Hold on," said Annie. "Are you sure we don't have time to run home real fast and get the folder for my project?"

"I'm sure," said Jack. "There's no way we can go there and then get back to school on time."

"Darn," said Annie.

"Remember you made a choice," said Jack.

"Right. I did," said Annie.

They passed the library and church.

"So what will you tell your teacher about your science project?" said Jack.

Annie frowned. "I'll just have to say I couldn't find my folder of pictures."

"I have a better idea," said Jack.

"What?"

He felt in his back pocket. The booklet from the Safari Ride was still there. He pulled it out and held it up.

"Show this to your class," he said. "Tell them about rhinos. And tell them about prehistoric rhinos. Tell them that present-day rhinos might disappear from the earth. Tell them that brave rangers, like Shani and Jomo, are trying to save them. Tell them the sad things and then the good things. That's your science project."

"Wow," Annie breathed. She took the booklet from Jack. "I really do have something to say."

"You have something huge to say," said Jack.

"I hope everyone listens," said Annie.

"They will. If you tell it the right way," said Jack.

By now, they were at the edge of the playground. The kids were still shouting and tossing balls and running races.

"Thanks, Jack," said Annie.

"Good luck," said Jack.

Then the bell rang.

Recess was over.

Here's a special preview of
Magic Tree House® #38
TIME OF THE TURTLE KING

Save the turtle king with Jack and Annie!

4

FLAMINGO LAGOON

Jack and Annie stepped off the pier. They walked up a sandy road into a small town.

They passed a few small shops: Seaside Gifts, the Green Lizard, the Tortoise Tavern.

"This isn't much of a town," said Jack. "It seems pretty empty."

"Maybe the active volcano is keeping most tourists away," said Annie.

"That's silly," said Jack. "The fisherman said it's completely safe here."

"True," said Annie. "But bad news can scare people."

"Stop," said Jack. He pointed at a sign marked WILDLIFE TRAIL. "There's the path that the fisherman told us to look for."

He and Annie left the road. They walked down a pebble path shaded by tree branches.

"Oh, wow! A pink iguana!" said Annie.

They stopped to look at a huge lizard resting on a branch. The iguana had pale pink skin with dark stripes.

"It looks like a tiny dinosaur," said Annie.

"The Galápagos are the only place on Earth where pink iguanas live," said Jack. "They've been here about five million years."

"I know," said Annie.

"Come on, there's the boardwalk over the lagoon," said Jack.

He and Annie headed over the raised wooden

walkway. As they crossed the murky water, they saw even more wildlife.

The dark pond was filled with ducks. Birds were cheeping and flitting everywhere.

"Mockingbirds, finches," Jack said.

"Herons and flamingos!" said Annie.

Blue herons stood in the shallows. A pair of flamingos waded together with slow, graceful steps. They dipped their heads into the water.

"They're like dancers taking a bow!" Annie said. She jumped up and down and clapped her hands. "Yay!" she shouted.

"Annie, you need to calm down," said Jack. "If you want people to see you as an expert, you can't act like a kid."

"Right, sorry," said Annie.

Jack and Annie left the boardwalk. They followed a short trail through a dry, mossy forest. The air smelled of mint.

Bright-yellow iguanas and long green lizards rested on tree trunks and branches. The whole island seemed alive with amazing creatures.

The forest soon opened into a clearing.

A one-story wooden building was bathed in sunlight. It had a thatched roof and a yard with fencing.

A sign said: GIANT TORTOISE CENTER.

"That's it!" said Annie. "A turtle expert's dream!"

"Right, but when we go inside, remember that experts act cool," said Jack.

"Cool is boring," murmured Annie.

"Yeah, but knowledge isn't," said Jack. "And we have tons of it."

As they walked up to the entrance, two white pickup trucks rolled into a parking area near the center.

"Oh, brother, it's the tourists from the Galápagos Cruises boat," Jack said.

"What's wrong with that?" asked Annie.

"I just hope they don't get in our way," Jack said.

"Don't worry," said Annie. "We don't even know what we're supposed to do yet."

Jack and Annie stepped into the lobby of the Giant Tortoise Center.

The lobby was filled with wildlife displays and a map of the building and grounds.

A tall young woman with a long black ponytail stood at a counter. She wore a green uniform and was quickly making notes as she talked to someone on the phone.

"Yes, sir, I understand," she said. "Emergency action was taken earlier today. But now they must try again."

What emergency action? Jack wondered.

The woman glanced up and saw Jack and Annie. They both pointed to their name badges.

The woman's eyes grew wide. "I have to call you right back," she said into the phone. Then she hung up.

"Welcome, Jack and Annie!" she said. "I'm Carmen, the only guide at the center right now. No one told me important guests were coming today. Our director should have been here to greet you. But we have an emergency—"

Before Carmen could finish, the tourist group from the boat banged through the front door.

Magic Tree House®

Magic Tree House®
Merlin Missions

Magic Tree House® Super Edition

Magic Tree House® Fact Trackers

More Magic Tree House®

Enough cool facts
to fill a tree house!

Jack and Annie have been all over the world in their adventures in the magic tree house. And they've learned lots of incredible facts along the way. Now they want to share them with you! Get ready for a collection of the weirdest, grossest, funniest, most all-around amazing facts that Jack and Annie have ever encountered. It's the ultimate fact attack!

Get whisked away again in the

MAGIC TREE HOUSE®

Graphic Novels!

Available now!